Stinky-Dog...
Where In The World Are You?

Written and Illustrated
by
LYNNE RUSSELL

Spidachio Press

For all my friends old and new,

The best of times I've had with you.

The worst of times you've seen me through,

And made me smile when I feel blue.

L. R. xx

First published in 2021 in the United Kingdom by Spidachio Press

Text and illustrations copyright © 2021 Lynne Russell

A catalogue record of this book is available from the British Library.

ISBN 978-1-9999840-9-0

Printed in the UK by
Biddles Limited, King's Lynn, Norfolk.

"Louie it's time for school," Mummy said,
"But please leave Stinky-Dog at home in bed."
Stinky-Dog felt sad on his own at home,
So he rang his friends on the telephone.

"Come over," he said, "we're going away.

Very faraway on a holiday!"

When the toys arrived he had found a trunk,

And now he was packing it full of junk!

"Where are we going?" Frog wanted to know.

"Some skis," Penguin said, "I think there'll be snow."

"A bucket and spade, we're off to the sea!"

Lobster squealed clapping his claws gleefully.

"We can see where to go using this map,"

Stinky-Dog said with the map on his lap.

"So many countries, which one shall we choose?

Snow, sea and sand or rocky mountain views?"

"I want to swim at the Pole in the South,"

Penguin declared with his long pointy mouth.

"Watch humpback whales breach in the icy sea,
And catch lots of fish to fill my belly!"

"The Australian seas are full of fish,"
Croaked Frog, "pack a knife, a fork and a dish.
Tropical fish in the Great Barrier Reef,
May bite you back with their serrated teeth!

"Jellyfish are a danger unforeseen,

Better to be safe in a submarine.

Or stay on dry land with a kangaroo,

Eating the veggies from his barbecue."

"The Bay of Bengal, how about that?

There's fish in the mangroves," said Stripey Cat.

Elephant trumped, "Then let me be your guide,

Through the forests of India we can ride...

"Past ancient temples, beauty to behold,

Shimmering in hues of pink, red and gold.

We can feast on the rainbow coloured fruit,

Found fresh in the markets along our route."

Lion roared, "Let's have tea with a chimpanzee,

On an African Wildlife Safari.

"We'll sail through the Sahara on the Nile,
Steering clear of the cunning crocodile.

"Stay away from the hippopotamus,

His tusks, teeth and temper are infamous!

From the Equator to the Cape of Good Hope,

We'll see zebra, giraffe and antelope."

"That sounds boring," Macaw squawked noisily,

"South America is the place to be.

I can soar through the air on a warm breeze,

Gorge on sweet seeds, nuts, leaves and berries.

"In the ruins, where the rainforest grows,

Hide howler monkeys and armadillos.

See snakes, jaguars, alpacas and llamas,

A myriad of bugs, birds and iguanas.

"Camp on the shores of Titicaca Lake,

Listen to crickets but watch out for snakes.

Sail from Bolivia onto Peru,

To climb through the clouds to Machu Picchu.

"Then leave behind that vast panorama...

And samba at Club Copacabana!"

"No...no!" Lobster cried, "I've got a notion,

We can all learn to surf in the ocean.

"Let's head west till we reach the Pacific.
I've heard the waves there are quite terrific!"

Rabbit groaned, "I don't want to go away
To Bombay, Zimbabwe or Paraguay.

"I know a place that we all will agree
Is the best by far of any country.
We don't need a boat, a bus or a train,
A submarine nor an aeroplane!"

"Okay," said Stinky-Dog, "then lead the way.

I'm fed up of packing, it's time to play!"

"Follow me," Rabbit said, "and you will see

Just how easy it is to be happy."

He took them outside into the garden.

The sky was bright blue, the sun was golden.

The air was sweet with a fragrant scent,

And all that old junk made a tiptop tent!

"You're right," said Stinky Dog, "I must agree,

We've had so much fun making this teepee."

"So," said Rabbit, "no need for such a fuss,

When all we need is here in front of us!"

"Whether we're in a land faraway,

Or just at home in the garden to play.

Even if it's only for a short while,

Being with our friends can make us smile."